TASTE THE MOON

ROBERT J. SODARO

Taste The Moon

A Novella By

Robert J. Sodaro

DARK FIRE PRESS
Ridgefield Park, NJ USA

Visit Dark Fire Press at
darkfirepress.com

Visit the Author's blog page at:
http://freelanceink.blogspot.com/

First Edition (POD): September 2025

ISBN: 979-8-9917012-0-4
ISBN (digital): 979-8-9917012-1-1

Dedication

We would like to thank Matt C. Ryan, the late Melvin Ylagan, and Rick Lundeen for Illustrating the initial comic adventures of the Wülf Girlz, and providing illustrations for this novella, and the trading cards.

Our thanks and appreciation also go out to J. M. DeSantis for agreeing to publish both the collected comic stories as well as this novella.

Special thanks goes out to Stephen R. Bissette for providing us with a most-excellent introduction, and we apologize to him for it taking 14 years for it to see print.

And finally, we would like to thank Martha for putting up with us and our antics as we assembled this and our other projects over the past several years.

—RJS
Norwalk, 2025

Cover to Wülf Girlz #1 (Dark Fire Press; 2023) © Melvin Ylagan

Preface

Stephen R. Bissette

As the cover[1] to this volume reveals, WulfGirlz, involves, well wolf girls—and the familiar visual cues are all in place.

Deep woods? Check.

Canine shadow, jaws agape? Covered.

Do we see an inverted pentagram (linked — in much lore, mythic, folkloric, literary, and cinematic — with the victim of a lycanthrope as much as the werewolf itself)?

Hey, that's not a heart with an arrow in it carved into that tree.

And consider the Wülf Girlz themselves, looking neither like Red Riding Hood, the archctypal "wolf girl" (as prey/potential victim), or like the scantily-dressed virgins and vampires that wandered amid Jean Rollin's distinctively dreamlike 1970s movies.

No, these Wülf Girlz fuse the glowering eyes of the alien fruit of John Wyndam's The Midwich Cuckoos, filmed as Village of the Damned (1960; the glowing eyes, BTW, were added to the US version only by its American distributor MGM) with the dress and body-language of the new Lolitas. What a generic tease, eh?

By all appearances, they are young, virginal, but something

---

[1] See cover to Wülf Girlz #1 on facing page.

other than human and (despite the lack of visible gore on the man presumably hanging from that tree behind them) apparently man-eaters. If I must continuously reference movies (I must! I must!), move over, Little Red Riding Hood; Hard Candy, here we come.

Grace and Hope are the Wülf Girlz, and as Robert J. Sodaro and Matt Ryan's first chapter makes abundantly clear, predators, beware. There's a lot more to Grace and Hope than is immediately apparent — to the other characters inhabiting Bob and Matt's invented comics universe herein, or to you, dear reader.

And that's what introductions are for.

Truth to tell, the history of horror comics are peppered with wolf women. Pre-Code horror comics thrived on domestic horror stories; as celebrated British media scholar, critic, and historian Martin Barker (A Haunt of Fears) discovered in his research into the British wave of Pre-Code horror comics, surviving records of publisher polls of their readership revealed more women read the damned things than did men.

That shouldn't be a surprise, given all the cheating husbands, murderous mates, and vengeful spouses that defined much of the Pre-Code comics realm, including the infamous and beloved EC horror comics Tales from the Crypt, Haunt of Fear, Vault of Horror, and the Crime-Suspense lines. The Pre-Code horror comics spoke clearly, precisely, and loudly to gender conflict and codes, and must have offered both a balm ("See, it could be worse") and cathartic vicarious thrills to the very generation of female readers who had just been forced to give up their newfound liberties during WW2, when most of the male adult population was drafted to wage war. The men returned (often traumatized and

shattered by their war experiences) to find households where roles had necessarily been inverted: women had been forced to become breadwinners, usurping the patriarchal "head of household" and tasting different lives, without their men or with other men or — well, no wonder the horror comics of the early 1950s spoke to a generation of women in ways no other media dared.

The "correction" of traditional gender roles was a major seismic fault in post-WW2 society, and the horror comics were filled with more wolf women than wolf men. Even as timid a horror comics publisher as National Periodicals (a.k.a. DC Comics) launched their tame "mystery" line with a wolf woman on the cover of the first issue of House of Secrets (cover dated January 1952, meaning it was on comics racks before Christmas of 1951 — before Christmas Eve werewolves could be born). Wanda Was a Werewolf was the cover story, a ravishing blonde beauty in a diaphanous gown literally running with a wolf pack, eyes blazing and blood-red tongues lolling out of gaping fanged maws. "Darling, forgive me, but there's no other way!" says her rifle-wielding man (husband? Beau?); of course, Wanda must be cut down. Doug can't have Wanda running around loose like that for long. "Wait, Doug!" his helpful, dressed- in-checkered-hunting-gear pal exclaims, "Only a silver bullet can destroy a werewolf!" In the reassertion of dominant male roles in the 1950s domestic equilibrium, one can never be too thankful for traditional male bonding over firearms (the hunters), and the wiser male friend harboring secret knowledge of women and lycanthropy who saves the day (the gatherer — of arcane knowledge of the wayward female).

"Werewolfism," as the idiots who articulated the newborn Comics Code in 1954 dubbed it, was firmly banned from four-color comics for almost a generation, save for the toothless humor comic mutts that occasionally popped up in The Adventures of Jerry Lewis or The Adventure of Bob Hope (both from National/DC). Female and male lycanthropes had to sit out the rest of the 1950s and the early 1960s as far as comics went, and it must be noted even

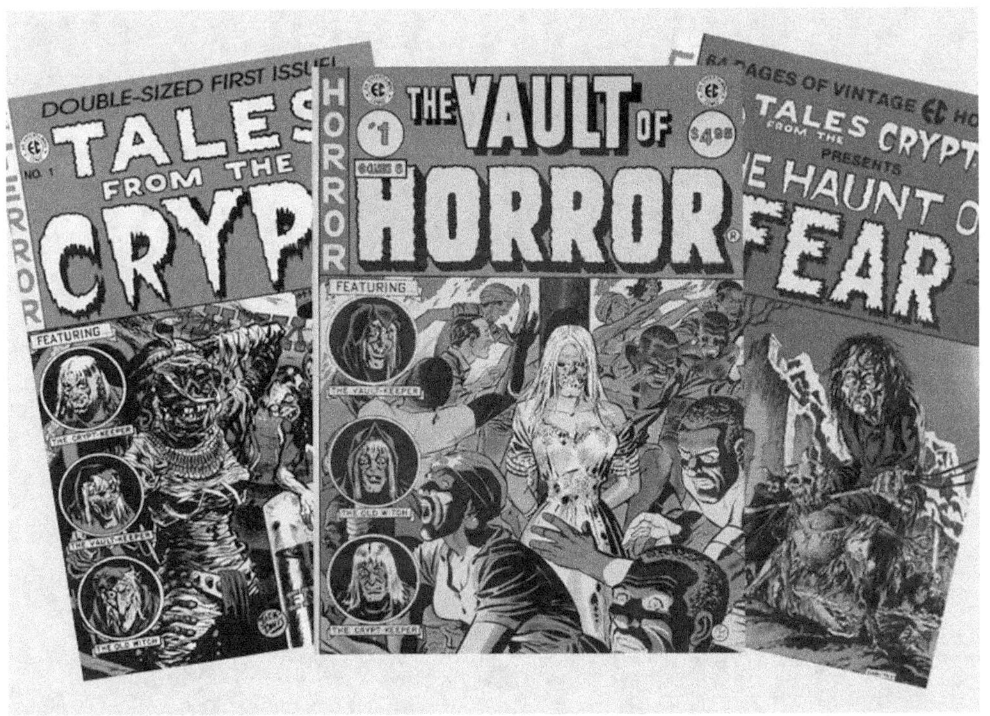

movies kept the archetype under wraps — after all, cat women were safer movie archetypes (the tragic "Panther Woman" in Island of Dr. Moreau, 1932; the even more tragic Irena in Jacques Tourneur/ Val Lewton's The Cat People, 1942). So, throughout this dry spell, drive-ins unveiled the rare cat woman (British Barbara Shelley's debut horror role in The Cat Girl, 1957; the "cat woman" of Roger Corman's faux-Poe feature The Tomb of Ligeia, 1964), but in Code-controlled comicbooks, even she took a back seat to all but the Batman's costumed foe of the same name. It wasn't until the 1965 rise of the Warren black-and-white horror newsstand comics zines Creepy and Eerie that wolf women howled anew for a new generation of comics readers.

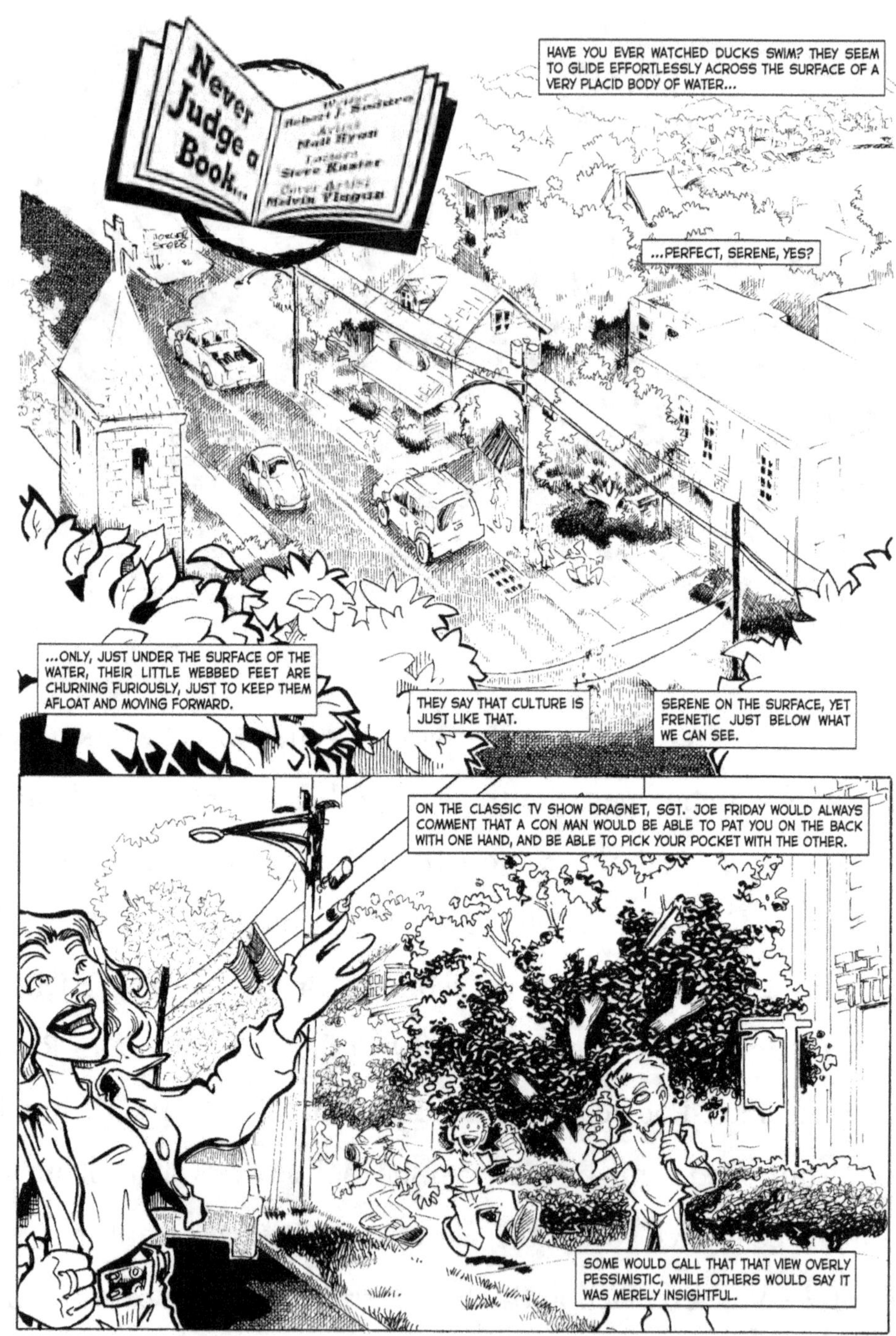

Page one from first Wülf Girlz story: © Matt Ryan.

Mythic archetypes as profound as the wolf woman do not take such lulls in the hunt for long. Comics and movies may have shunned the wolf woman, but they were still out there to be read and fed. The reprints of classic texts by British clergyman and scholar Montague Summers (1880–1948) — The History of Witchcraft and Demonology (1926), The Vampire: His Kith and Kin (1928), and particularly The Werewolf (1933) — kept alive the venerable folklore of the female lycanthrope. Herein, she was an unholy incarnation of ravenous, unleashed sexuality: the timeless assertion of primal male dread of female power, which fit the disposition and prejudices of clergyman Summers like a fist in a hunter's glove.

Thankfully, the wolf woman changed, as shapeshifters must. She blossomed anew in the wake of the sexual revolution of the 1960s and '70s. The counterculture's guilt-riddled adoration of Native American cultures added momentum to the archetype's revival — wolves, women with wolves, and wolf-women were now a positive, empowering archetype — as did the 1970s feminist revolution. With the underground wimmen's comix movement, cartoonists like Trina Robbins (who designed the costume for Vampirella, Creepy, and Eerie's sister, for publisher Jim Warren and character creator Forrest J. Ackerman) made heroines of animal-women: Trina's Panthea was an early icon of the scene. In literature, key texts like Angela Carter's The Bloody Chamber (1984) revitalized and reinterpreted venerable texts and archetypes: Little Red Riding

Hood's relationship to and with the Big Bad Wolf was never the same thereafter, as this past year's harvest of revisionist fairy tale movies (including Red Riding Hood, 2011) prove. Carter (1940-1992) was no less a prominent British scholar and writer than Summers had been in his day, arguably moreso, and she had no patience with the patriarchal codes, repressions, and gender stereotypes of early 20th Century culture: with The Bloody Chamber, she ushered in a brave new world of woman, wolves, and wolf women.

I could also cite books like Clarissa Pinkola Estes's Women Who Run With the Wolves: Myths and Stories of the Wild Woman Archetype (Ballantine, 1992) or the more down-to-earth biographical account of Tanja Askani's Kinship with the Wolf: The Amazing Story of the Woman Who Lives with Wolves (Park Tree Press, 2006), but I won't. I'm frankly more interested in the female shapeshifters, which brings us — at last! — back to the Wülf Girlz. As you shall see in Chapter One of Wülf Girlz, Grace and Hope may look frail and vulnerable, but they are to be feared.

The wolf woman has been a more fearsome (to males) archetype in films than lycanthropic cinema would infer. Does anybody remember femme fatale Louise Glaum, who blistered the screen in 1916 as The Wolf Woman, an emotional "maneater" giving heady competition to Theda Bera's more iconic Vamp? No? Well — huh, I thought not, but nevertheless, there she was — and from The Wolf Woman of the silent era to the Egyptian/Arabic rarity Nesaa Wa Zeaab/ Women and Wolves (1959/1961), the linking of woman and wolf to denote latent savagery and the metaphoric (and at times literal) baring of sexualized fang and tearing of claw has remained in fashion. The association gained new momentum in the savage '70s, giving rise to the sadistic Ilsa: She-Wolf of the SS (1974) and her Nazi sister compatriot in Andre Delvaux's Een Vrouw Tussen Hond en Wolf/Woman Between Wolf and Dog (1979,

costarring a youthful Rutger Hauer). I could go on, embracing the loopier lucan metaphysical mania of Sze Ma Peng's Jin Fen You Long/Venus the Ninja/ Wolf-Devil Woman 2 (1983), but you get the idea. All manner of ravenous "wolf women" have plagued put-upon male heroes, anti-heroes, and villains alike, particularly during times of war (WW2 being a particularly fertile time frame, in men's magazines and semi-pornographic sex/gore movies) when gender roles up-end and women in power ruthlessly masticate menfolk, so to speak.

Enter, then, Grace and Hope—wolf women of a new generation—who most obviously owe a debt to their more immediate contemporaries.

Look, I could go on and on and on. I could argue (as comics fans, reviewers, and critics no doubt will) that the breakthrough that spawned Wülf Girlz came with the Canadian horror sleeper

Ginger Snaps[2] (2000), wherein sisters Brigitte (Emily Perkins) and Ginger (Katharine Isabelle) were divided by "the curse" (pun intended, as in scripter Karen Walton and director John Fawcett's original story). Being a wolf woman still had its downside, sure, but was also liberating in ways it had never been before. "You love it," Ginger tells her little sister Brigitte as lycanthropy unleashes the wolf within. "Should come for the ride. A little scratch. Swap some juice. We'll be our own pack, like before. It's so 'us,' B." Indeed.

Lest the debt to Ginger Snaps be too strongly asserted (after all, Chapter Two does echo and reference the 19th Century Canadian setting for the prequel Ginger Snaps Back: The Beginning, 2004), I must remind you that Wülf Girlz is just beginning here — Bob and Matt are just getting warmed up.

Let's see whcre they take us.

There's already plenty of fresh blood on view, to my eyes and taste.

Selfishly, I'm also gratified to note that Grace and Hope are Vermonters — which, I suspect, is why I was asked to write this introduction in the first place. Vermont is my native state, mind you, home to poet and underground comix (and Star Wars comics) writer Tom Veitch, and cartoonists like his brother Rick Veitch, as well as Ed Koren, Frank Miller, Alison Bechdel, Harry Bliss, and

---

[2] For the record we (Bob Sodaro) didn't see the film, or its sequels until long after we conceived of, and wrote these initial stories.

many others, including our first-ever state Cartoonist Laureate, James Kochalka. I think Wülf Girlz might fit into that grand tradition just fine; they've got plenty of brothers and sisters in ink, if not blood.

Grace and Hope are sisters, yes, but they also have comicbook sisters. Among their absolutely immediate contemporaries in comics are the delightful vegetarian werewolves Hallie and Ellen writer/ artist Betsey Swardlick introduced in the pages of the anthology Werewolf ! (2008), Failwolves. Betsey's comedic Failwolves (who are hilarious instead of horrific; sisters, not competitors, to the Wülf Girlz) have grown as characters through three issues of the title (Werewolves!! and Werewolves!!!, natch — which, by the way, just happened to have been originally edited and published in Vermont), just as I've no doubt Grace and Hope will continue to grow as Bob and Matt continue their collaboration.

To quote another wolf woman I cited just above:

> "Should come for the ride.
> "A little scratch.
> "Swap some juice.
> "Join the pack…"
>
> Come on.
> Let's howl!

— Stephen R. Bissette.
Mountains of Madness, Vermont; April (July 2011)

Page from 2nd Wülf Girlz story: © *Matt C. Ryan.*

Illustration by Rick Lundeen

Taste the Moon
(A Wülf Girlz Tale)

Everything was a blur. Grace was running, running hard. Her breath was coming in ragged gasps. There was a stitch in her side. She felt as if she had been sprinting for an hour, even though she knew that simply couldn't be true. Why couldn't she remember, she was with Hope and Papa Jacques by the campfire. Then there was the pain and the blood.

Wait. The wind shifted and there was a new sent. No, that wasn't right. She heard a branch snap ahead and off to her left. She could feel rather than sense her sister, Hope pacing her own pell-mell rush just slightly off her right side. Grace knew better than to look. Hope was there, Hope was always there, and she was running just as hard as was Grace. Plus, her little sister's unrequited joy of the chase that Grace could tell that her little sister was having the time of her life.

Crashing through the wooded underbrush she could tell that someone (something) was ahead and off to the left — not the quarry, something other. Still, she was running flat out, all four (wait, four?) legs churning up the ground. Her sleek, black fur (fur?) matted back against her skull. Her ears pressed flat back: her lips curled back exposing her gleaming fangs.

Then she broke through into a clearing. There. In front of her was her prey. A young buck, only just coming into his points. He was backed against a large thicket, unable to retreat any further, he had chosen to stand and fight. Needless to say, that would prove to be his undoing.

The buck put his head down, shook it, pawed the ground, and snorted. Grace curled her lips back and uttered a low, menacing growl. Her yellow teeth glinting in the pale light of the gloriously full Moon. The buck then brought its head up to look towards Grace. It was at that moment that Hope's lithe, lupine form came flying out of the wood at the buck. There was no finesse in her attack; it was all bluster and fury, but it somehow managed to work.

In fact, it was the sheer force of her projectile attack

that allowed her to bowl the buck over, rolling it onto its back. The creature's legs flailed as it vainly attempted to right itself and kick its attacker into submission. Even though she had sensed the presence of her younger sister, and had anticipated the attack itself, Grace was still momentarily thrown off her own attack.

Not wanting to disappoint Papa Jacques, she quickly reassessed the situation. Hope was on her back; teeth firmly embedded in the back of the neck of the buck. Meanwhile, with the much larger buck lying on top of Hope, shifting and squirming as it attempted to shake loose its pint-sized attacker. Grace had one shot, and seeing her opening, took it. She dove at the buck's exposed neck, baring her fangs she tore out a big chunk of the buck's neck.

As she landed on the far side of the dying beast, she turned her head back to watch as a river of blood pumped out of the creature's carotid artery and spill all over her sister and onto the ground. The beast shook violently as it entered its death throes, then it twitched, and stopped moving.

Grace disentangled herself from the dead moose, reared herself back on her haunches, and let out a pitched, mournful cry, seeing her older sister baying triumphantly over their kill; Hope scrambled to her feet and likewise began howling in harmony with her sister. Together their baleful moan reverberated across the hillside and throughout the wood.

Their lament done the two wülf pups turned their attention to their kill and set themselves to devouring the carcass. For the next several minutes all that could be heard in the glade was the feral sounds of an extraordinary repast. Once satiated the two girlz, thoroughly covered in the ichor and gore of the beast, began to settle in for the night.

Grace walked in a small circle and settled herself with her back to a tree. Once she was settled in, Hope crawled over her sister and snuggled up next to and protected by Grace. There the two lupine sisters lay, fed and secure in the knowledge that they had just committed their first solo kill under the tutelage of their Papa Jacques.

An hour or so later a shift in the wind, a stray sent, a subtle shift in the depths of the wood that Hope couldn't quite name caused her to lift her head. She wasn't alarmed so much as she was aware of the change. Sleepily, she lifted her head and slowly scanned the Moon-lit glade. At the furthest edges of her senses, where the wood broke, she again felt rather than saw a shadowy familiar figure.

"Papa Jacques," she mouthed even though her lupine jaw couldn't quite properly form around the words themselves.

"Sleep, little one," came a voice in her head. "Sleep well, for you did your Papa proud tonight."

Even across the glade she could feel his love and approval, and she settled back into the bramble around her. Sleepily, and without waking, Grace nuzzled closer to the protective warmth of her elder sister.

***

It was the evening of the Moon following the Moon of the night of the big kill. Grace was again running through the deep wood. She was again on the scent of an unlucky prey. This time — even though she was galloping along at full tilt she had no stitch in her side. Her breath came in an even measure, and she had a reserve on which she could call if need be.

Off to her right and slightly ahead of her, flanking and herding was her sister, loping gracefully along, always aware of the presence of the quarry. Shepherding it to its appointment with its destiny. Grace's easy gate ate up the Moonlit trail as she closed in upon her prey. He was near. She could feel its fear, taste its panic.

Then it turned and rushed her from around the base of a stand of trees. The big buck came crashing back towards her. A month ago, this reversal might have caught her unawares, but Grace, bless her black little heart, had already caught the prey's change of direction, and begun her charge early.

Grace halted her own charge, bared her fangs, uttered a low growl and prepared to leap. The buck reacted to the change in her demeanor just as Grace expected, which put him completely vulnerable to Hope's flying leap. As could be expected, the buck was so focused on the full-frontal assault by Grace that he totally missed that she wasn't working alone.

Hope's flying attack was as swift as it was silent. She executed her killing strike on the buck as if she had been killing prey for years rather than a couple of months. In the seconds before she too propelled herself towards the hapless quarry, she quietly marveled at how far they had come from where they had once been. The rustic calm and quaint charm of Vermont seemed like a 100 years rather than a few months ago.

The thrashing death throes of the buck brought Grace back. She spotted her opening and launched herself at the hapless creature, latching her jaw onto the beast's underbelly, and ripping through muscle, bone and sinew as she delivered the killing blow. The three of them rolled around in the glade for another minute or so as the two girls ripped and clawed away at the dying buck. Once it was dead, they disentangled themselves from the dead creature's carcass and threw back their heads in unison. They then howled their triumph to the fullness of the Moon. Long and loud, they proclaimed their triumphant kill. The Moon was their father, the Moon was their mother, the Moon was their sister and brother. They were The People and this was their kill. This was their legacy.

Their wailing ended, they set themselves to the task of their kill. After the chase they were ravenous, and they fed with gusto. Then, their hunger satiated, they prepared to settle in for the night. Once again, Hope held back as her elder sister padded down a bedding of leaves and grass, situating herself with her back to a large rock. This done, the smaller wülf snuggled up to her and almost immediately fell asleep. Hope secure in the protection of her sister, and Grace secure in the knowledge that Papa Jacques was close by.

Just beyond the edge of the clearing, at the edge of the wood where he lay, Papa Jacques, his young charges were coming along quite well. He was proud of his girls. They were coming into their new heritage quite well. It was not very long since their first Moon. They were both natural hunters and took to The Way better than he had seen in an age. Come the morning, he knew that he would begin the next phase of their training.

It was well past dawn when the first rays of dawn cracked the leafy canopy of the small glade. As the light slowly illuminated the underbrush a pair of young girls at the far end of the glade began to stir. The pair of them were covered in the gore of the beast they had killed and devoured the night before. Hope slowly opened her eyes and surveyed the area around her. Her younger sister, Grace, was still asleep in her arms, where she conked out the night before.

Grace sniffed the air and could still sense the presence of Papa Jacques. A second sniff told her that there was someone else out there as well. She wrinkled her forehead as she attempted to place the scent. Then she got it, it was always harder to properly get a sent in human form. It was Rosalie. Nudging her sister Grace started to stretch. "Come on, sleepyhead; time to wake up, daylight's burning."

Hope sighed and stirred slightly. Grace jostled her younger sister harder. "Come on Hope, I'm not kidding, move it."

Hope only buried the curly golden locks of her hair deeper into her older sister's lap, refusing to allow herself to be awakened. Needless to say, her older sister refused to take 'no' for an answer, and simply jostled the younger girl harder.

"Come on, I can smell Mama Rosalie coming."

Reluctantly, Hope slowly opened her eyes and smiled at her sister. "Mornin'"

Grace kissed Hope's forehead and then playfully pushed her away. "You have a piece of fur in your teeth."

"Yeah, well you have moose breath."

"T' bot' o' you stink ta high Heaven, an' ya surely need baths," came the lilting, lyrical voice of a fine-looking Jamaican woman, black as the night with eyes that contained the laughter of the world.

"Mama Rosalie!" Both girls squealed at once, jumping to their feet as the matronly woman wearing a long flowing, brightly colored, flower print dress that fell to her ankles entered the glade.

"Have you girls no shame? Standin' out here in da open nakid as the days you were born and covered in the gore of the beast ya killed last night."

Both girls giggled uncontrollably as they hugged each

Illustration by Rick Lundeen

other. "Yea we kilt that moose real good, Mama Rosalie," Grace said. Grace was 10 with long straight brown hair, while Hope who was nearly eight with equally long, though wavy blonder hair. Both were slim, with Grace standing a couple of inches taller. That they were sisters was immediately obvious to anyone who would look at them. Both had alabaster skin, which was darkening with a growing tan that indicated that they spent much of their lives outdoors in the sun.

"And he tasted real good too!" Hope chimed in, a broad grin on her face.

"Shameless!"

A slight movement at the edge of the tree line captured the attention of the three females, and Mama Rosalie hurriedly reached into the mesh bag she was carrying. She tossed each of the girls a formless dress that they each quickly pulled over their heads.

No sooner than they were properly covered than a strapping Black man with a wild main of heavy dreadlocks flying about his head came striding into the glade. "Now wat's goin' on here?" He asked as if he had not a care in the world.

"Papa Jacques! Papa Jacques!" Both girls cried out as they launched themselves towards the fellow. As they reached him both became impossibly airborne and flew the last couple of feet towards him, wrapping their arms and legs around the hapless fellow, nearly bowling him over with the shear velocity of their friendly assault.

Papa Jacques, who was by now used to their combined flying attack bravely endured the twin flying, squirming missiles, standing tall as they nuzzled the well-muscled Black man. After a moment when they settled down Jacques turned his attention to Rosalie who looked on both lovingly and disapprovingly at the same time.

"An' you're gonna wanna be sain' sumthin' disaprovin' an' all now, I'm-a bettin' now," Jacques said with a twinkle in his eye and genuine mirth in his voice."

"An' why would I be sayin' anythin' about you lettin' dese young girls stayin' out all night by demselves, an' in the altogether to be sure."

"It's not like ya didn't know what you were gettin' in ta when ya agreed ta help me raise dese girls," Jacques countered as he stepped closer to Rosalie.

"Sure, an' dat makes everytin' OK, eh?"

"Not OK, but ya shudda had some idea o' what to expect, den..."

Jacques' voice trailed off as he allowed some faint disturbance just off the outer edge of his senses to distract him. A half second later Grace caught the scent, followed by Hope. The three of them turned sharply towards the presence with Jacques taking point and the girls instinctually falling into flanking positions even though they weren't in wülf form.

"Rosalie, get behind us, quickly!" Jacques hissed.

Still unaware of the imminent danger, she hesitated, confused by the flurry of activity. It wasn't until the three men wearing animal pelts stepped into the glade did she realize what was going on, and quickly moved behind Jacques and the girls.

The three men were very muscular and well-tanned, with a feral look about them that indicated they lived life hard, took what they wanted, and had little tolerance to those who stood in their way. Rosalie became very fearful of the safety of the girls and herself.

The three men seemed to simply appear out of the

forest; one in the center and the other slightly forward and well-spaced apart on either side of him, close enough to protect his position, yet far enough away so as to not be caught up in any attack that could take down more than one of them.

"Nice to see you, Islander," the man in the center said to Jacques in a tone that indicated that the meeting was anything but accidental. His accent and facial features betrayed him as an old worlder from beyond the Asiatic rim.

"Nice to see you, Mongol," Jacques mimicked warily, his eyes taking in the entirety of the scene in front of him, even as his other senses reached out in an attempt to determine what else was going on around them that he couldn't see.

"Taking your new family out for a morning stroll, are you now, brother?" The Mongol said as he and his two wingmen as one, all took a single step closer to Jacques and his family.

"I'm no brudda ta da likes o' you, Mongol, an' I'll thank ya ta keep yer distance now."

The trio halted their advance. "No, I'll say you're not,

especially given that you seem to be inducting wülflings into the clan, and you know that's not right," the Mongol said menacingly.

"I know da code, Mongol, I'm on my way to council now, to say my piece before them, an I'm bringin' my girls wit me."

"Then you should rejoice, for your judgment is at hand, brother, for the mountain comes to you. The Council will be here tonight, and your transgressions will be judged by the full of the Brethren at the height of the new Moon." The Mongol and his guard all took another step closer in unison.

From behind Jacques a branch snapped, and Rosalie gasped.

Without altering her gaze at the three men in front of them Grace whispered, "Papa Jacques!"

"Hush, darlin'," Jacques responded as he reached his hand back, lightly touching the arm of his stepdaughter, his eyes unwavering from the tableau in front of him. A smile played with the edges of his mouth as he watched the trio of men in front of him react to what was occurring behind him.

"Just remember, Mongol, you are not de only one wid friends in dese wood."

The Mongol hissed at Jacques, spun on his heal, and disappeared into the wood. Caught in the unexpected turn of events, the other two men found themselves leaderless, and also swiftly retreated to the relative safety of the wood at the far end of the glade.

Jacques and his stepdaughters allowed for the passage of a couple beats of time before allowing themselves to relax and turn to view what was transpiring behind them. What they saw was half a dozen swarthy-looking men spread out in a semicircle behind Jacques lead by a very determined-looking woman with a shock of flaming red hair that was desperately attempting to escape a deep green bandana. Behind the semicircle of men, hovering just inside the tree line of the wood beyond the glade was the hint of a shadow of a dozen more potentially hostile figures.

Rosalie was standing stock still, both of her hands covering her mouth with a look of shock and awe on her face, facing the flame-haired woman. Jacques gently put his hands protectively on Rosalie's shoulders and gently whispered in her ear, "Don worry Rosalie, dese are my very good friends."

Jacques then slid past the matronly woman and approached the younger red-haired woman and said, "Leave it ta you ta made da most dramatic entrance possible, m'love."

"Och, an' leave it to ya t'git inta as much trouble as humanly possible." She scolded in a lilting Irish brogue that took the sting out of the words themselves. Then she took a step closer to Jacques and quite literally flung herself into his arms, her legs wrapping themselves around his powerful torso, even as his arms snaked around her slim waist.

The two young girls giggled uncontrollably as the two adults nuzzled. When the young firebrand finally let Jacques come up for air, he seemed to recall his young charges and gingerly allowed his lady to slip back to the ground. Once her feet were firmly planted on the good Earth, he formally addressed the issue at hand.

"Scarlett, as well ya know, we've been apart near two years. In that time there've been some changes. M'darlin' daughter Lilly was tragically taken from me, recently, but da good Lord saw fit to allow me da opportunity an' privilege to raise a pair o' daughters in da life."

With one arm around Scarlett's waist, Jacques turned towards his family and introduced them. "Dese are ma stepdaughters, Grace and Hope, an' dere nanny, Rosalie." Each of females gently curtsied as they were introduced. Scarlett acknowledged each of them in kind then whirled towards Jacques as the enormity of his words struck home.

"Are ye mad?" She exclaimed. "Ya brought these wee ones into the Clan! Then that's the reason that Kahn wants yer head. It's the one rule dat none of us ever break. Ya ken that!"

"It was an accident," Hope interjected, a tear coming to her eye. Papa just went to talk, but the men were angry because of the cows and one of the men shot Lily by mistake."

"Papa Jacques didn't mean to hurt us." Grace chimed in, "we were trying to help Papa. Then we ran away but the bear found us and we...we...changed..."

Scarlett looked at the two youngsters. Rosalie moved closer to the girls, standing behind them, a hand on each of their shoulders as she looked at Scarlett. "Da girls were traumatized, by what happened, so was Jacques. Now we're family, an' dat's dat."

Overcome with her own emotions Scarlett got down on her knees and hugged the children. "Fear not wee ones, we're all family here now, an' our family takes care of its own."

A moment later she stood and looked at Jacques. "So now we should go ta meetin' place and get ready for E's arrival."

Several hours and many miles later Jacques and his small clan arrived at a particular stand of trees when they stopped, and Jacques turned to face Rosalie. "Rosalie, ya kno ya can't go any farther, Roscoe an' Evan will take ya back a ways for safety."

Without a word of protest, Rosalie turned to face each of the girls and hugged them each in turn. Then, accompanied by the named fellows, they was escorted back into the wood. The rest of the group moved forward with the girls holding each other's hands.

A hundred yards further into the wood they stopped abruptly. The girls crowded close to their stepfather as Scarlett moved protectively closer. The gloom of dusk causing an even deeper shade of gray to wash over the stillness of the wood. A pair of formidable-looking sentries dissolved from the overgrowth and barred their path.

"Who dares to come to this place and presumes to stand before the Council?" One queried.

"I am Jacques Dumont, of the People of the Moon, I was born in 1805 on the Isle of Jamaica on the shore of the great ocean, and I canna die. I seek to stand in presence of our elders and make me case in the presence of all to hear."

"Jacques Dumont, of the People of the Moon, from the Isle of Jamaica, you and your clan may proceed, but you must divest yourselves of all weapons before entering the circle of Elders."

After complying, Jacques and his party silently slid forward like the ghosts they were. Arriving to the outskirts of a fair-sized bonfire where they stopped again, just on the periphery of the light cast by the fire. A look from Jacques caused most of those who traveled with him to take up positions around the western portion of the fire (knowing that those with the Mongol would be positioned around the eastern part); only then did Jacques, Scarlett, and the girls enter the ring of light.

Situated with the bonfire behind them were five tree

stumps that served as seats. On each of those seats was a clan elder. Jacques, Scarlett, and the girls stood in front of them facing the seats and bonfire. The girls, not knowing quite what to expect, resigned themselves to watching the proceedings.

"Before Brother Moon rises this eve we will deal with the proceedings before us," one of the elders said.

"Brother Jacques," another of Elders began, "You have gone against one of our most sacred rules and inducted wülflings into the fold of the people. Perhaps even after the decade you've been among our number you still think as the humans do?"

"Ya kno' dat' not so, Brother Joseph."

"So then, Brother Jacques, if you understand the code of the people, why then are there uninitiated wülflings here, among us?" A third elder inquired.

"Yes, Brother Jacques," came a distinctive voice, thick with the flavor of the old world, "tell us why you think so little of the laws that govern us."

A murmur rippled through the assemblage as every head spun about to locate the source of the new voice, which so clearly did not come from one of the elders. The hushed tones grew louder when the owner of the voice stepped out of the dark of the wood and into the circle of light cast by the fire.

The hooded figure walked slowly, leaning slightly on a gnarled cane, and flanked by a pair of powerful men. Defying convention the one called the Mongol stepped forward and challenged the hooded figure. "Who are you, and how dare you interrupt our proceedings?"

The figure considered for a moment the arrogant man standing in front of him, turned towards the Elders, then back to the Mongol. Slowly the figure raised both hands and drew back his hood, revealing his features for all to see. A gasp ran through the crowd. Even the Mongol appeared surprised and took a step back.

"Elijah!"

The silver-haired Elder at the center of the five stood and swiftly moved to stand in front of the Council. The girls looked at each other, then at Scarlett. Realizing their confusion, she knelt between them and pulled them in close.

"He is Elijah, the oldest of the People. He's never before been in the new world."

Before the Elder could speak to Elijah, the older man waved him to silence, and tuned to Jacques, motioning him forward. Jacques took a half step towards Elijah, stopped and turned towards the girls. "Come." He said, and they hurried to his side. Together they walked close to the old man.

"Dese are my daughters now, Brother Elijah, if you are to ban dem, den I go too. If you mean ta harm dem, ya have ta go tru' me."

An audible gasp flowed through the group, as no one ever dared speak to an Elder like that, especially one so august as Elijah. The old man, more ancient than any could recall, stared intently at the insolent pup that was Jacques Dumont, then at his children. Then he threw his head back and let loose a long and hearty laugh.

"Well, you certainly have a big brass set on you for such a young wülfling."

"It was my own rage dat orphaned dem, so it is my responsibility ta raise dem rite."

"So true it is, my young friend." Raising his voice for all to hear, "Let all of the People be so honorable as our brother Jacques." Elijah then looked at Jacques "Go with

Illustration © Rick Lundeen

your woman, tonight your daughters will run with me."

Jacques hesitated for a moment, but Elijah reached out and put a reassuring hand on Jacques's arm. "Fear not my brother. I will watch over them as if they were my own pups."

Again, raising his voice to speak to the assembly Elijah said, "So, now that our brother the Moon has risen, let us all take our true forms, and run with abandon." With that he threw back his head and let loose a howl that could be heard by all.

As the girls watched in awe, an incredible transformation came over the seemingly frail form of the aged man before them as he morphed into the powerful form of a silver-furred lupine wolf. Taken by the change of the Elder first Grace, then Hope, followed by Jacques, Scarlett, and all the rest of the People each got lost in their own transmographacation.

Once in their true state, the two wülf girlz paired off with the great silver wülf that was Elijah and loped off into the wood. Their stepfather watched them blend into the night, then turned and accompanied by a flame-red wülf went off in a different direction.

The girlz had no trouble keeping pace with the silver Elder as he took them on long run through the wood. Finally, after a couple of hours they stopped, and drank from a stream. No sooner did Grace put her head down to drink than she lifted it again, her ears perked up, and the fur on the back of her neck began to bristle. A low growl alerted the others.

Elijah sniffed the air and took off to the west with the girlz close behind. The three wülves came to a low bluff and peered to the clearing below. At the foot of the overhang, they saw the Mongol and two other wülves cruelly baiting a bear cub. It was obvious even to the two wülflings that they were torturing it before the kill.

They had the cub surrounded on three sides, each taking a swipe at the small creature while it was distracted by the others. It was clear they had been doing this for some time and were wearing the cub down by minute amounts in order to extend the kill.

In fact, they were so intent on their game they missed what both Grace and Hope saw coming. The cub's father, an enormous black bear emerged from the wood behind one of the Mongol's escorts and, with one massive paw swatted the wülf with a mighty blow that sent it flying into a nearby tree. A loud crack as the wülf struck the tree made and a piteous whimper indicated that the creature's back snapped on impact.

The two remaining wülves immediately turned their attention on the larger bear as the cub collapsed in exhaustion. The Mongol charged directly at the bear as his companion attacked from the bear's right. Unfortunately, the Mongol's feint didn't have the desired effect as the bear's swipe caught him along the side of the head, knocking him into his companion spoiling his assault as well.

His timing off, the bear was able to avoid the second wülf and gut it with a swipe of his paw before turning his attention back to the Mongol who was still dazed from the hit he took.

Without waiting for confirmation, Grace, followed half a heartbeat later by her younger sister, leapt down the embankment and charged into the fray. With little concern for their own safety the girls, snarling and growling, galloped headlong towards the fighting beasts.

In spite of the fact that there was no time to coordinate their attack, the months that they had worked together under Jacques paid off, as Hope dropped back a half a stride and drifted slightly to the right as they raced forward. Just as they got within striking distance of the bear, he managed to tag the Mongol for a second time, knocking the wind out of him.

The bear was so intent on the Mongol that the rapid appearance of a snarling Grace directly in front of him threw him off. As he directed his attention at her lithe form and swung a mighty blow at her she easily ducked beneath his swing as Hope approached undetected from his flank and took a bite out of his side.

Roaring in pain, the bear redirected his attention towards Hope who had already dropped back out of his reach, which allowed Grace to rake her claws across his unprotected belly. Surprised by the audacity of the frontal assault the bear turned back to Grace. As could be expected Hope used the distraction to make another strike.

Utilizing this two-pronged, asynchronous attack pattern — always careful to alter their angle and direction of attack — they were able to inflict terrible damage to the bear all the while dancing frustratingly just beyond his reach. Still, even with their superior speed, agility, and psychically attuned attack pattern it was only a matter of time before the bear would get lucky and catch one of them.

Fortunately, that moment never arrived as a good 10 minutes into their blitzkrieg assault, Elijah sprang from behind the bear landing square on the larger beast's back, his claws digging deep into the flesh of the bear; his powerful jaw clamping hard on the back of the bear's neck.

Enraged, the beast rose up on his hind legs as he tried to shake Elijah from his back. The girlz took that opportunity to attack together, biting and clawing for all they were worth. Confounded by the multiple points of attack the bear was momentarily vulnerable to the killing strike that was delivered by the Mongol who had recovered enough to return to the mêlée as he dove straight for the bear's juggler, ripping it out in an audacious assault.

That was all the bear could take and it collapsed under the combined fury of the four wülves. As the massive bear hit the ground it lost any advantage it might once have had and the four wülves ripped into him swiftly tearing him to shreds. Within moments it was all over, and the bear was dead.

Breathing hard the four wülves, each covered in the gore, blood, fur, and body parts of the bear disentangled themselves from the dead creature. Grace, her eyes bight from the kill leaped up on top to the bear's fallen form lifted her head and let loose a long mournful howl proclaiming her kill and stating her dominance.

No sooner had Grace bayed her reverence to the Moon than her sister leapt up beside her and echoed he sister's proclamation. Soon Elijah's and the Mongol's voices were added to the blood chorus. The sounds of their cry reverberated through the wood, crashing over and over throughout the night.

Once the cacophony subsided Hope, as the youngest, put her head down and tore off a chunk of meat and dropped it in front of Elijah, then nosed it closer to the Elder. However, before he could pick it up and eat Grace became aware again. Something was amiss. She looked around then discovered what it was. The cub had recovered and was now moving.

The Mongol's lips curled back over his sharp, yellowed teeth and a throaty growl emerged from his throat as he took a step towards the young bear, only Hope moved to block access. At first the Mongol looked quizzically at her, and then he understood. Lumbering out of the wood came another black bear, this one not so massive as the one they slew, but large enough.

The Mongol, still growling, took a step towards this new intruder, but this time it was Grace that blocked his approach. The new bear reared up on its hind legs and made threatening sounds at the wülves but didn't approach. Instead, it came down on all fours and, with one eye on the wülves, moved towards the cub.

This then was the cub's mother.

Wary of each other's presence, and under the tacit protection of the girlz, the mother bear coaxed her cub to the far side of the clearing and into the wood. When the Mongol was satisfied that the bears had moved on, he turned back to Elijah, who signaled that it was now safe to eat, and the wülves fed.

Satiated, Grace and Hope moved off to bed down for the night; while the Mongol and Elijah took up flanking positions and also bedded down.

At first light Grace awoke, her sister curled up in her arms. Grace looked about and spotted Elijah sitting nearby, grinning. He stood and walked towards the girls. He had fashioned himself a kilt out of the bear's pelt. "Here," he said, tossing a pair of pelts towards the girlz. "Put these on, we have a ways to walk to get back to the pack."

Grace pulled one of the pelts around herself as she nudged her still slumbering sister with one foot. "Where's the Mongol?" She inquired.

"I sent him on ahead," Elijah said, "to let your Papa know you are safe, and to give me a little more time to get to know you girlz. There is a creek just over that rise to our south." Elijah said as Hope got dressed. "We can clean up a bit before we get on our way."

It was then that Hope asked Elijah the question she had been harboring since she had first seen him. "Are you Eliyaho?"

Stunned, Elijah looked down at the youngster. "Y-you mean the prophet Eliyahu?" Elijah stammered. "Why would you think that?" He asked.

"Scarlett said you are the oldest of the People, and that you came from the old world."

"But why...?"

"Our real Papa was a preacher, and he always read to us stories from scripture," Grace chimed in.

"No, my daughters," Elijah said, smiling, I'm not the prophet your Papa told you about. I'm old, but not nearly that old. Now come we need to be off." And the trio headed off towards the stream.

The sun was high in the sky when the three happy, but weary travelers arrived back at the encampment. As soon as the girls spotted Jacques, they raced towards him, launching themselves in his direction as was their customary welcome.

At once they both began to excitedly tell him about the previous night's adventure. Alternating the narration from one girl to the other as they each told a different perspective in their shared telling of the story. Jacques dutifully nodded his head back and forth between the girlz as he listened to their tale.

When they finally wrapped the story, Jacques put them both down and bade them go off with Scarlett to get lunch. So, they ran off to get fed and re-tell of their adventure all over. As soon as they were off Jacques turned to the Elder. "So, dey account well for demselves?"

"Truly, brother Jacques, in all my days on this Earth, I've never experienced a pair of wülflings so attuned to the rhythms of the Moon or with each other. Tudor them well, my brother, and they will well enhance the story of the People."

"Aye, Islander. I tell you true," the Mongol said as he approached, "I was ready to deny them entry, but I tell you now that anytime they choose, they can run with me."

"Actually," Came Grace's young girl voice from behind the Mongol. The men turned to see both girls standing with plates of food. "Perhaps, given enough time, you might be good enough to run with us."

"But don't hold your breath waiting," chimed in Hope as she shoveled food into her mouth.

The Mongol stared openly at the two young ladies then let loose a hearty laugh. "I know that these are your daughters not by blood, Islander, but they surely have inherited your big brass pair already!"

"Truly, dat dey have, Mongol, dat dey have," Jacques responded glumly pleased to be resigned to his fate as their new father.

The following night, Grace again ran with wild abandon, Hope, as always, to her right and slightly behind. Leading tonight, however, were Jacques and Scarlett. The four ranged far and wide knowing that while more tests of their prowess would surely come, the most important one had already been passed. They were a part of the People.

Jacques led his small family up the long sloping rise of the mountain, past the tree line to the very crest of the pinnacle itself. Once there, at the crest he stopped' threw back his head and howled reverence to the Moon. His soulful baying was picked up and carried by Scarlett, Grace, and Hope as each attained the summit.

When their song ended Jacques lead them to a protected enclave and they all settled in for the night, their bodies intertwined with each other for comfort, heat, and protection. As each drifted off to sleep, Jacques allowed himself one more glimpse at the Moon hanging high overhead and fell asleep secure in the knowledge that if there was one thing that he could be assured about these, his once and future children, it was that they could most assuredly taste the Moon.

# # #

Afterword

Come with me on a little walk of shameless self-promotion and fond, but melancholy remembrance. It was the summer of 2006 when a former professional associate of mine, reached out to me in a phone call and extended to me a wonderful invitation, he wanted me to contribute to a horror anthology comicbook entitled **Psychosis!** from a comicbook he was co-publishing for a group called Guild Works Productions.

As it turns out, he was interested in producing a horror comicbook anthology that was different from the kinds of horror anthologies that had previously been published. The idea for **Psychosis!** was that the comic was designed to be a 56-page, black and white, horror anthology where the main theme was that of an edgy, modern-day, relevant look at the fears of the 21st

Panel from first WülfGirlz story: © *Matt C. Ryan.*

Unused cover for Wülf Girlz © Melvin Ylagan

Century. Not so much Vampires, zombies, and werewolves (oh my!), but things that truly frightened us, here, now, in the 21st Century. To be sure, we did in fact have some actual (iconicly classic) monsters — most notably my own Wülf Girlz — but the challenge was to write stories that truly frightened us as individuals. As a father, I chose this.

That call came to me in the middle of the day with the instruction that my contribution was needed, well ASAP, if not sooner. Flattered, I very politely declined. stating that not only was I not really a fan of horror, but I hadn't written anything in a year, and had not written fiction in 10 years, so I totally wasn't the person for this project. Hence, I begged off, saying that I had to go pick my son up from his job, and that I would call back later. As it turned out, in the short period of time it took me to go pick my son and return home (less than an hour), I had hit on an idea, which I pitched in a return call when I got back home.

Oddly enough my idea was approved, and I was told to write it up. I took the next two weeks to write. It was an eight-page story, and the first six pages took me a week to write and then another week to write the concluding two pages (the story's climax). The story was that horrific to me. It was my story, but it frightened me. It was the tale of a pair of children out in the world (presumably) unprotected from the terrifying monsters that occupy the world around them. By now you know that Grace and Hope are a pair of pre-adolescent girls who were (inadvertently) bitten by a werewülf in 1856, and then never aged beyond their chronological ages.

Shortly after the book came out in 2006. I was sitting at a horror convention where I first Melvin R. Ylagan, the artist who illustrated one of the variant covers for the issue (the one that spotlighted my characters). As he was reading the story, Melvin asked me when I was going to write a follow-up story. I told him that it was a one- off, and that there would be no follow-up story. Melvin insisted that there had to be one and I said that it was a one-trick pony. Given the way the story was constructed (the Girlz weren't revealed as being werewolves until the end of the story), you now knew the "trick," and I couldn't pull it again. Melvin went on to insist I was wrong, stating that there had to be more stories as the girlz themselves stated that they had been bitten 150 years earlier.

This time it took me less than five minutes to be inspired. Of course, there were more stories to tell, there was the

Panel from 1st WülfGirlz story: © Matt C. Ryan.

story of how they became werewülves, which naturally suggested the follow-up story of how they went from werewülves to werewülves who stalk pedophiles. With this in mind, we've gone from a standalone story to a graphic novel, to a (hopefully possible) movie; and now we're off to the raccs. It was from that plotting session that I

Panel from 1st WülfGirlz story: © Matt C. Ryan.

was able to craft the origin story of the Wülf Girlz (which appeared in issue #3 of **Psychosis!** — the story about how they became hunters of predators was subsequently written (and illustrated by Rick Lundeen in 2012) but never appeared in print with the original publisher, but — several years later was published in color by InDELLible Comics, 2020). Two additional Wülf Girlz scripts have been written (but not illustrated), while another 20 or so stories have been plotted out.

Early on, while I was waiting for more comicbook stories to be published from the original publisher, I chose to write a prose story, so I did. (As a complete aside, I wrote the complete text of the story that appears in this print edition, as a pair of very long text files on the cell phone I was then using (circa 2007). I then transferred it to my computer where I edited and refined the tale.)

Panel from 3rd WülfGirlz story:
© Rick Lundeen.

As to where Steve Bissette comes into all of this, in 1987 I met Steve at a comic con in New Hampshire. At the time, I was a freelance writer contributing to

Amazing Heroes (among other fan publications), and Steve had just announced that he was putting together a horror anthology entitled ***Taboo***. I told Steve that I'd like to interview him about the project, and then went back to my editor over at ***Amazing Heroes***, Kim Thompson, and pitched the story, which was well received. However, when I went back to Steve, he indicated he wasn't quite ready to publish, so I went back to Kim and relayed this information. Kim told me that was okay — as he really wanted the story — and when I did get the interview, to let him know, and he would schedule the piece. Well, once a month or so for a year, I reached out to Steve, to inquire if he was ready to publish. Finally, he was ready, and we sat down to a four-hour interview (which started out by me explaining to him that I really don't much like horror and wound up with it turning out that I knew about 90% of the horror references that he made, be they print, TV, or film) and which eventually did appear in *Amazing Heroes #153*.

Then, for the next decade, whenever I would run into Steve, he would not only enthusiastically greet me, but then introduce

me to everyone around him. I never really understood why he was being so nice to me (other than Steve really **is** a nice guy), until one time, when he told everyone in his group that I was the first person to write about *Taboo*, and then suddenly everything clicked into place. Well, time passed, and I eventually lost touch with Steve. However, after the publication of the *Wülf Girlz* stories, I sought him out to tell him that I had finally crossed over to his side of the desk and had written a horror story. When I decided that I wanted to publish a longer-form, standalone volume of Wülf Girlz ('07/'08), I asked Steve if he would pen a forward, to which he graciously agreed.

All of which brings us to 2019 where I ran into an old friend, J.M. DeSantis, publisher of Dark Fire Press at the FIT Diversity con in NYC. J.M. reminded me that shortly after the initial appearance of the Wülf Girlz, he wanted to team his character, Chadhiyana up with the Girlz. A story I had started, but never finished. This discussion lead to us discussing the possibility of

Panel from 3rd WülfGirlz story: © Rick Lundeen.

Dark Fire actually publishing the Wülf Girlz (and me finishing off the team-up story). Well, J.M. was enthusiastic about publishing the Girlz, and I promised to actually write the team-up (something I'm still intending to do). Well, it has taken nearly 19 years since the original idea of a standalone Wülf Girls comic, but it looks like that tome has finally seen print under the Dark Fire banner. I want to (once again) thank Matt C. Ryan (the original artist), Melvin, and Rick for participating in producing the comic, I want to thank Steve for graciously contributing the forward of this novella (then patiently waiting all these years for it to appear in print), I want to thank J.M. for being willing to publish both the comic and this novella, and I want to thank all of you who not only picked up this prose novella of mine about the Girlz, (and hopefully the comic as well), but for, you know, reading this far.

Robert J. Sodaro,
Connecticut, 2018 (updated 2020, & '25)

On the three following pages are a pair of Wülf Girlz short stories that were written by Robert J. Sodaro and illustrated & © by Rick Lundeen.

STRAIGHT
OUTTA
DA WOODS

'NITE, PAT!
NIGHT.
THE LAST BUS IS LONG GONE, LITTLE LADY.
NOT WAITIN' ON NO BUS.
NO?
BIG SISTER, GRACE, WENT TO FIND DINNER.
WHERE? DINER'S CLOSED.
DUMPSTERS, BEHIND THE DINER.
DON'T SEEM RIGHT, PRETTY YOUNG THING LIKE YOU EATIN' OUTTA A DUMPSTER.
WE RUN OFF FROM HOME. GOTTA EAT SOMEWHERE.
HOPE, DINNER.
IT'S GONNA BE COLD TONIGHT. I'M NOT FAR FROM HERE, YOU GIRLS WANT TO SPEND THE NIGHT WITH ME?
OK
WHY'D YOU GIRLS RUN AWAY FROM HOME?
MOM MADE DAD LEAVE, THEN SHE GOT DRUNK AND FELL DOWN THE STAIRS.
THEY WERE GOING TO SPLIT US UP AND PUT US IN FOSTER HOMES, SO WE LEFT.
STOP
DINER

CLICK!
SO, WHAT SAY YOU GIRLS AND I PLAY A LITTLE GAME?
IS IT ANY FUN?
WELL I REALLY LIKE IT.
HOW DO WE PLAY?
WELL FIRST, WE HAVE TO TAKE OFF ALL OUR CLOTHES...
HUH?
I HAVE A BETTER IDEA, HOW 'BOUT WE JUST KILL YOU IN THE MOST PAINFUL WAY POSSIBLE, AND EAT THE REMAINS, YOU SICK TWIST?
DIDN'T ANYONE EVER TELL YOU? THE YOUNG ONES ARE WEREWÜLVES!
NOOOO! PLEEEEEASE!!
GROWL!
WÜLF GIRLZ IN:
"IT HAPPENED ONE NIGHT..."
STORY: SODARO • LUNDEEN :ART
WülfGirlz - Tearing it up in a comic shop near you!
© 2010, Robert J. Sodaro/Freelance ink & Rick Lundeen/Epoch

STORY:
BOB SODARO
HOPE & GRACE
:ART
RICK LUNDEEN

WHAT'S THAT OVER THERE?
A TIRE.
NO, NEXT TO IT. IT LOOKS LIKE A TO-GO CONTAINER.

WHATCHA DOIN'?
GETTIN' DINNER.
IS THAT A PIZZA BOX?

HEY THERE SWEETIE, AREN'T YOU A CUTE THING?
WHAT COULD BE BETTER THAN HALF A PEPPERONI PIZZA?

ACTUALLY, I CAN THINK OF SOMETHING BETTER.
I CAN THINK OF TWO SOMETHINGS.
ME TOO, WHAT SAY WE ALL GET BETTER ACQUAINTED, EH?

I HAVE A BETTER IDEA.
HOW 'BOUT WE KILL YOU TWO IN THE MOST PAINFUL WAY POSSIBLE..
...AND DINE ON YOUR REMAINS! YOU SICK TWITS...

CRUNCH
SNAP

DIDN'T ANYONE EVER TELL YOU? THE YOUNG ONES ARE WEREWÜLVES!

Adventures of the Wülf Girlz

War of the Independents

44

Transformed by the accidental bite of a werewülf, sisters Grace & Hope now spend their lives defending others from predators & monsters.

Wülf Girlz

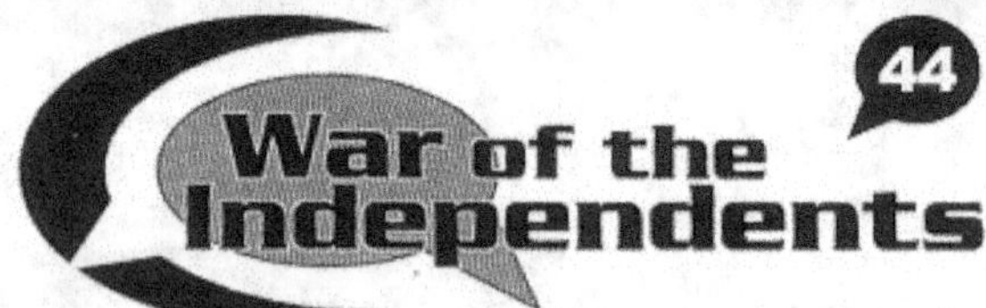

First App- Psychosis! #1 (2006)
Art : Rick Lundeen
Writer: Robert J. Sodaro
www.freelanceink.blogspot.com

Mock-up Wülf Girlz art for the War of the Independents trading cards (Part of the Phazer trading Card Set); illustrated by Rick Lundeen.

NOW AVAILABLE

OUR FIRST LAUNCH OF 2025!

FROM PUBLISHER